The route to your r

When they look back at their formative years, many Indians nostalgically recall the vital part Amar Chitra Katha picture books have played in their lives. It was **ACK – Amar Chitra Katha** that first gave them a glimpse of their glorious heritage.

Since they were introduced in 1967, there are now **over 400 Amar Chitra Katha** titles to choose from. **Over 90 million copies** have been sold worldwide.

Now the Amar Chitra Katha titles are even more widely available in **1000+ bookstores all across India**. Log on to www.ack-media.com to locate a bookstore near you. If you do not have access to a bookstore, you can buy all the titles through our online store **www.amarchitrakatha.com**. We provide quick delivery anywhere in the world.

To make it easy for you to locate the titles of your choice from our treasure trove of titles, the books are now arranged in five categories.

Epics and Mythology
Best known stories from the Epics and the Puranas

Indian Classics
Enchanting tales from Indian literature

Fables and Humour
Evergreen folktales, legends and tales of wisdom and humour

Bravehearts
Stirring tales of brave men and women of India

Visionaries
Inspiring tales of thinkers, social reformers and nation builders

Contemporary Classic
The Best of Modern Indian literature

Amar Chitra Katha Pvt Ltd

© Amar Chitra Katha Pvt Ltd, 2003, Reprinted October 2012, ISBN 978-81-89999-83-4
Published & Printed by Amar Chitra Katha Pvt. Ltd., Krishna House, 3rd Floor,
Raghuvanshi Mill Compound, S.B.Marg, Lower Parel (W), Mumbai- 400 013. India
For Consumer Complaints Contact Tel : +91-22 40497436
Email: customerservice@ack-media.com

The route to your roots

INDRA & SHIBI

It is little wonder that Indra was the lord of all gods – he displayed the true characteristics of a perfect leader. It was his diligence and eye for detail that ensured that only the virtuous were given god-like status. Arrogance and impatience were soon corrected. But, most importantly, as a leader, Lord Indra strove to be worthy of his position.

Script
The Editorial Team

Illustrations
H.S.Chavan
And
Dilip Kadam

Editor
Anant Pai

Cover illustration by: Pratap Mulick

INDRA AND SHIBI

SHIBI RAJA WAS RENOWNED FOR HIS VIRTUE. SO FAMOUS WAS THIS KING, THAT EVEN THE DEVAS CAME OUT OF THEIR CELESTIAL ABODE TO WATCH HIS YAJNAS ⊕

WHEN HE COMPLETES THAT YAJNA, THE LARGE-HEARTED KING WILL ATTAIN THE STATUS OF A DEVA.

INDRA, KING OF ALL THE DEVAS, AND AGNI, THE GOD OF FIRE, OVERHEARD THESE REMARKS.

I WOULD STILL TEST THE KING AND WOULD BESTOW BOONS UPON HIM, IF HE PROVES TO BE THE NOBLEST OF KINGS.

⊕ FIRE SACRIFICE

I, TOO, WILL GO WITH YOU. I AM CURIOUS.

A FEW DAYS LATER —

O KING, SAVE ME!

NOW, NOW. STOP TREMBLING. I AM HERE TO PROTECT YOU.

GIVE UP THAT BIRD, O KING. IT IS MY PREY.

I CANNOT, MY FRIEND. IT HAS SOUGHT MY PROTECTION. I CANNOT FORSAKE IT.

YOU ARE KNOWN TO BE A VIRTUOUS KING. IS WHAT YOU SAY IN ACCORDANCE WITH DHARMA?

I AM A KING. IT IS MY DUTY TO PROTECT THE WEAK.

I TOO NEED YOUR PROTECTION. I AM HUNGRY. IF I DO NOT EAT, I WILL DIE.

IF I DIE, MY WIFE AND OUR FLEDGELINGS WILL PERISH. AS YOUR SUBJECTS WE, TOO, SEEK YOUR PROTECTION.

O KING, PLEASE DO NOT GIVE ME UP!

I WON'T, LITTLE ONE. DO NOT FEAR.

WILL YOU LET ALL OF US DIE TO SAVE ONE CREATURE?

WHAT HE SAYS IS CORRECT.

WILL OUR KING GIVE UP THE PIGEON?

NO! HE WON'T! HE WILL GIVE UP HIS LIFE. BUT THE PIGEON—NEVER!

YOU WON'T HAVE TO STARVE. YOU CAN HAVE AN OX, A BOAR, A DEER OR A BUFFALO...

WHAT WILL I DO WITH THEM? THEY ARE NOT THE NATURAL FOOD OF HAWKS! I AM A BIRD OF PREY AND I PREY UPON PIGEONS.

THEREFORE, O RIGHTEOUS KING, RELEASE THE PIGEON FOR ME.

I'LL GIVE YOU ALL THAT I HAVE, MY KINGDOM TOO. BUT NOT THIS PIGEON, WHICH HAS SOUGHT MY PROTECTION!

AS THE ASSEMBLY WATCHED WITH BATED BREATH —

O KING, IF THE PIGEON MEANS SO MUCH TO YOU, CUT A PIECE OF FLESH FROM YOUR RIGHT THIGH EQUAL TO THE WEIGHT OF THE PIGEON.

I SHALL GO AWAY SATISFIED WITH YOUR FLESH.

WHAT A CRUEL ALTERNATIVE!

BUT SHIBI RAJA DID NOT THINK SO.

O GENEROUS HAWK, YOU DO ME A GREAT FAVOUR.

AND CUTTING OUT HIS FLESH, SHIBI RAJA WEIGHED IT AGAINST THE PIGEON.

OH! THE PIGEON IS HEAVY! I WILL HAVE TO GIVE SOME MORE OF MY FLESH.

SHIBI GAVE UP PORTION AFTER PORTION OF HIS FLESH BUT THE PIGEON WEIGHED MORE.

ALAS! HE IS BARE TO HIS VERY BONES. WHAT WILL HE DO NOW?

LOOK!

HE'S STEPPING ON THE SCALE!

LET'S STOP HIM! IS THE KING TO BE SACRIFICED FOR A MERE PIGEON?

LOOK! THE HAWK HAS VANISHED!

AND SHIBI BECAME WHOLE AGAIN.

THE NEXT MOMENT —

O KING, I AM INDRA. THE PIGEON WAS NONE OTHER THAN AGNI. WE WANTED TO TEST YOU AND WE FIND YOU JUSTLY FAMOUS.

YOUR NAME SHALL REMAIN IMMORTAL ON EARTH; AND A PLACE WILL BE KEPT FOR YOU IN HEAVEN.

INDRA, KRISHNA AND UTTANKA

INDRA WAS ONCE BUSY TALKING TO KRISHNA. SUDDENLY HE STOPPED.

HE WAS A TRIFLE ANNOYED.

WHAT'S THE MATTER, KRISHNA? YOUR ATTENTION WANDERS. WHAT ARE YOU THINKING ABOUT?

OH! ABOUT SAGE UTTANKA. A FEW DAYS AGO, I REVEALED MY-SELF TO HIM IN MY VISHWAROOPA* AS HE MEDITATED IN THE DESERT.

* COSMIC FORM OF KRISHNA IN WHICH ALL THAT EXISTS IS SEEN WITHIN HIM

"I OFFERED HIM A BOON."

THAT I HAVE BEHELD YOU IS BOON ENOUGH, O KRISHNA!

"WHEN I INSISTED, HOWEVER —"

IF I MUST, THEN LET ME HAVE WATER WHEN-EVER I NEED IT. FOR WATER IS SCARCE IN THESE DESERTS.

SO BE IT. WHENEVER YOU FEEL THIRSTY, THINK OF ME.

HE IS THINKING OF ME NOW. HE IS AN ENLIGHT-ENED SOUL. I WAS WONDERING...

WHAT?

WHY NOT GIVE HIM AMRIT INSTEAD OF WATER?

NO, KRISHNA, NO. AMRIT, THE NECTAR OF IMMORTALITY, IS FOR THE DEVAS ALONE. WHY DON'T YOU GRANT HIM SOME OTHER BOON?

HE DESERVES NOTHING LESS. DO NOT STOP ME, INDRA.

ALL RIGHT. IF HE MUST HAVE AMRIT THEN LET ME TAKE IT TO HIM.

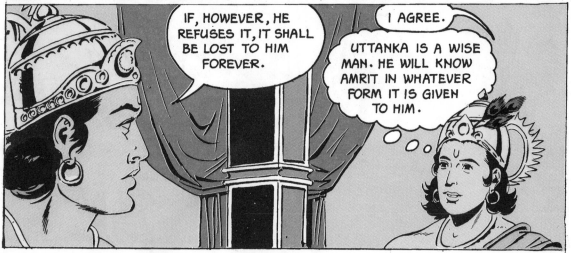

IF, HOWEVER, HE REFUSES IT, IT SHALL BE LOST TO HIM FOREVER.

I AGREE.

UTTANKA IS A WISE MAN. HE WILL KNOW AMRIT IN WHATEVER FORM IT IS GIVEN TO HIM.

MEANWHILE, UTTANKA WAS STILL THINKING ABOUT KRISHNA.

SUDDENLY —

FOOTSTEPS! IT MUST BE KRISHNA BRINGING ME WATER.

TO HIS DISMAY HE SAW A CHANDALA* APPROACHING HIM.

UTTANKA, I COULD NOT BEAR TO SEE YOU TORTURED BY THIRST. I HAVE BROUGHT SOME WATER FOR YOU. PLEASE ACCEPT IT.

UTTANKA WAS AGHAST. HE SHRANK AWAY FROM THE CHANDALA.

MY THROAT IS PARCHED WITH THIRST. BUT HOW CAN I ACCEPT WATER FROM HIM! O KRISHNA, WHAT A CRUEL JOKE TO PLAY ON ME!

* AN OUTCASTE

11

WHY DO YOU HESITATE? DRINK, UTTANKA, LEST YOU DIE OF THIRST.

UTTANKA FLEW INTO A RAGE.

WHAT! ACCEPT WATER FROM A CHANDALA! BEGONE! I'D RATHER DIE OF THIRST THAN TOUCH THAT WATER AND BE POLLUTED!

THE NEXT MOMENT THE CHANDALA HAD VANISHED.

BEFORE UTTANKA COULD COLLECT HIMSELF — WHO SHOULD STAND BEFORE HIM BUT KRISHNA!

OH, KRISHNA! IT WAS NOT FAIR TO SEND ME WATER THROUGH A CHANDALA!

THAT WAS NO CHANDALA. IT WAS INDRA BRINGING AMRIT FOR YOU. NOW YOU WILL NEVER RECEIVE IT IN THIS BIRTH!

AND KRISHNA TOLD HIM ALL ABOUT HIS BET WITH INDRA.

HE WHO DISCRIMINATES BETWEEN A BRAHMAN AND A CHANDALA DOES NOT DESERVE AMRIT.

PARDON ME, LORD.

YOUR FAULT HAS BEEN GREAT. YET MY BOON WILL NOT BE WITHDRAWN.

WHEN YOU ARE THIRSTY, CLOUDS WILL RISE OVER THIS DESERT AND GIVE YOU WATER TO DRINK. THEY SHALL BE KNOWN AS THE UTTANKA CLOUDS.

I AM GRATEFUL TO YOU, LORD.

AND TO THIS DAY, UTTANKA CLOUDS RISE AND SHOWER RAIN ON THE ARID DESERT.

INDRA AND THE ASURA KING

IN THE DAYS OF YORE, THE DEVAS AND ASURAS WERE EVER AT WAR, FIGHTING FOR SUPREMACY OVER HEAVEN, EARTH AND THE NETHER REGIONS. ONE DAY, A VIRTUOUS ASURA KING CAME TO AMARAVATI, THE CAPITAL OF INDRA, KING OF THE DEVAS.

INDRA WAS PERPLEXED.

HE IS THE SWORN ENEMY OF OUR RACE. YET HE COMES ALONE AND UNARMED!

SOON THE PERPLEXITY TURNED TO ALARM. THE ASURA SEEMED TO HAVE A STRANGE EFFECT ON THE DEVAS.

WHAT'S THE MATTER WITH THEM? THEY SEEM TO BE ENCHANTED BY HIM!

HOW CALM AND CONFIDENT HE IS!

THE STRANGE LIGHT EMANATING FROM HIM ENVELOPES US IN ITS WARMTH!

INDRA SUDDENLY FELT VERY WEAK.

THEY ARE BOWING BEFORE HIM, IGNORING ME, THEIR KING.

NOT KNOWING WHAT TO DO, INDRA QUIETLY GOT UP...

...AND LEFT THE ASSEMBLY.

OUR KING! HE'S DESERTING US.

STOP HIM!

DO NOT PANIC. I SHALL RULE OVER YOU AND PROTECT YOU.

AND THUS THE ASURA BECAME MASTER OF THE THREE WORLDS.

MEANWHILE —

I MUST GET TO THE SECRET OF THE ASURA'S STRANGE POWER.

A FEW DAYS LATER, A BRAHMAN STOOD BEFORE THE ASURA KING.

I WISH TO BECOME YOUR DISCIPLE, O VIRTUOUS KING.

I HAVE NO TIME FOR YOU, O BRAHMAN. I AM BUSY RULING OVER THE THREE WORLDS.

16

MAY I AT LEAST LISTEN TO YOU WHEN, IN YOUR MOMENTS OF LEISURE, YOU CHANCE TO SPEAK ON CONDUCT?

HE IS A DETERMINED MAN. HE WILL MAKE A GOOD DISCIPLE.

YES. YOU MAY. I SHALL ALSO TRY TO FIND TIME TO TEACH YOU.

AND I WILL WAIT UPON YOU AND SERVE YOU AS MY GURU.

THE BRAHMAN DULY TREATED THE ASURA AS HIS GURU AND WAITED UPON HIM HAND AND FOOT.

WHAT AN EXCELLENT DISCIPLE! HIS EAGERNESS IN LISTENING TO ME IS MATCHED ONLY BY HIS HUMILITY IN SERVING ME.

IN THE COURSE OF HIS LEARNING, THERE WAS ONE QUESTION WHICH THE BRAHMAN PERSISTED IN ASKING.

HOW WERE YOU ABLE TO WIN OVER THE THREE WORLDS? TELL ME, O KING, WHAT MEANS DID YOU USE?

MY UNQUESTIONING OBEDIENCE TO SHUKRACHARYA, MY PRECEPTOR. MY ACTIONS ARE BASED ON HIS PRECEPTS.

ALAS! I CAN'T SAY THAT I HAVE ALWAYS TAKEN THE ADVICE OF MY GURU, BRIHAS-PATI!

THE BRAHMAN WAS QUIET FOR A WHILE. THEN —

DO YOU ALWAYS OBEY SHUKRA-CHARYA? EVEN IF HIS ADVICE GOES AGAINST YOUR WISHES?

19

SO IT WAS BY YOUR RIGHTEOUS CONDUCT ALONE THAT YOU MASTERED THE THREE WORLDS.

AND SO WELL DID THE BRAHMAN CONDUCT HIMSELF, THAT ONE DAY—

I AM HIGHLY PLEASED WITH YOU FOR YOUR DUTIFUL BEHAVIOUR. ASK OF ME ANY BOON AND IT WILL BE YOURS.

THE BRAHMAN COULD NOT BELIEVE HIS GOOD LUCK.

IF THAT IS YOUR WILL, I WILL OBEY YOU.

HIS CONDUCT LEAVES NOTHING TO BE DESIRED. HIS VERY ACCEPTANCE OF THE BOON IS IN OBEDIENCE TO ME.

COME, TAKE WHAT YOU WISH.

THEN LET YOUR SPOTLESS CONDUCT BE MINE...

... THAT IS THE BOON I PRAY FOR.

HE DOES NOT ASK FOR COWS OR GOLD AS ANY POOR BRAHMAN WOULD.

IT IS YOURS!

HE HAS SURPASSED ALL IN KNOWING THE ESSENTIAL. I AM PLEASED THAT HE HAS ACQUIRED THE SENSE OF TRUE VALUES BUT...

... I AM FILLED WITH DREAD. HE IS NO ORDINARY BRAHMAN. WHO COULD HE BE?

AS SOON AS THE BRAHMAN WAS GONE —

A DEEP ANXIETY NUMBS MY BEING. I DO NOT KNOW WHAT TO DO.

21

THE ASURA SAT BROODING. SUDDENLY —

THE ASURA WAS STARTLED.

WH-WHO ARE YOU?

I AM THE EMBODIMENT OF YOUR SPOTLESS CONDUCT. GIVEN AWAY BY YOU, I DWELL IN THE BRAHMAN HENCE-FORTH.

AND THE FORM VANISHED.

WHAT HAVE I DONE!

I, TOO, SHALL GO TO THAT BRAHMAN.

WHO ARE YOU?

I AM RIGHTEOUS-NESS. I LIVE WHERE SPOTLESS **CONDUCT** LIVES. I MUST LEAVE YOU.

AS SOON AS RIGHTEOUSNESS VANISHED, A THIRD FORM EMERGED FROM THE ASURA.

I AM **TRUTH**. I SHALL LEAVE YOU, FOLLOW-ING THE WAY OF RIGHT-EOUSNESS.

WHEN TRUTH VANISHED—

I AM THE EMBODIMENT OF **GOOD DEEDS**. I CANNOT LIVE WITHOUT TRUTH. SO I FOLLOW TRUTH.

AND GOOD DEEDS, TOO, VANISHED.

THE NEXT MOMENT ANOTHER FORM EMERGED FROM THE ASURA, WRITHING AND ROARING AS IF IN PAIN. FOR A MOMENT THE ASURA FORGOT HIS OWN PREDICAMENT.

O BEING, WHY DO YOU CRY? WHO ARE YOU?

I AM **POWER**. I LOVED TO RESIDE IN YOU BUT I AM COMPELLED TO FOLLOW GOOD DEEDS.

THE NEXT MOMENT —

WHO ARE YOU, O RADIANT ONE?

I AM THE GODDESS OF **PROSPERITY**. WITHOUT POWER I HAVE NO LIFE...

...AND HE DEPENDS ON GOOD DEEDS! SO I SHALL HELP HIM FOLLOW THE WAY OF GOOD DEEDS — TO THE BRAHMAN.

WAIT, O GODDESS! BEFORE YOU GO, TELL ME THE TRUTH. WHO IS THAT BRAHMAN?

HE IS INDRA, KING OF THE DEVAS.

INSTRUCTED BY YOU, HE KNEW THAT IT WAS BY YOUR CONDUCT ALONE THAT YOU CONQUERED THE THREE WORLDS.

SO, WHEN YOU OFFERED HIM A BOON, HE CHOSE YOUR CONDUCT RATHER THAN COWS OR GOLD.

FOR HE LEARNT FROM YOU THAT IF YOUR CONDUCT WERE HIS, THEN RIGHTEOUSNESS, TRUTH, POWER AND PROSPERITY TOO WOULD NATURALLY BE HIS.

COME, OUR LORD AWAITS US.

MEANWHILE INDRA ASSUMED HIS TRUE FORM AND...

...ONCE AGAIN GAINED SOVEREIGNTY OVER THE THREE WORLDS.

OUR LORD SEEMS TO BE ENDOWED WITH A NEW RADIANCE!

THE GLOW THAT EMANATES FROM HIM ENVELOPES US IN ITS WARMTH.

INDRA AND YAVAKRITA

IN THE DAYS OF YORE, THERE LIVED TWO SAGES WHO WERE CLOSE FRIENDS. ONE OF THEM WAS A RENOWNED VEDIC SCHOLAR AND THE OTHER, AN ASCETIC.

WHILE THE SAGES LOVED AND RESPECTED ONE ANOTHER, YAVAKRITA, THE SON OF THE ASCETIC, WAS AN UNHAPPY SOUL.

MY FATHER'S ASCETICISM HAS BROUGHT HIM NOTHING, WHILE THE VEDIC SCHOLAR IS HONOURED BY ALL.

I SHALL PRACTISE SEVERE PENANCES AND BY PENANCE ALONE SHALL I MAKE THE FULL KNOWLEDGE OF THE VEDAS MINE.

27

THE POWER OF MY PENANCES SHALL BE SUCH THAT THE CELESTIALS WILL BE COMPELLED TO GRANT MY DESIRE.

SO GOING TO THE BANKS OF THE GANGA, HE LIT A SACRIFICIAL FIRE.

TILL ONE OF THE CELESTIALS APPEARS BEFORE ME TO GRANT MY DESIRE, I SHALL EXPOSE MY BODY TO THIS FIRE.

AT AMARAVATI, INDRA WAS DISTURBED BY YAVAKRITA'S PENANCES.

I MUST FIND OUT WHY HE IS TORTURING HIMSELF SO!

SO HE APPEARED BEFORE YAVAKRITA.

WHAT DO YOU HOPE TO GAIN BY SUCH SEVERE AUSTERITIES?

LORD, I WANT KNOWLEDGE OF THE VEDAS DEEPER THAN THAT OF ANYONE ELSE.

THEN WHY DON'T YOU SEEK A GURU?

A GURU WOULD TAKE SEVERAL YEARS TO IMPART SUCH KNOWLEDGE TO ME. I CAN ACQUIRE IT FASTER BY THE STRENGTH OF MY PENANCE.

THE WAY OF PENANCE IS NOT THE PROPER WAY. GO AND LEARN THE VEDAS FROM A GURU.

AND TO YAVAKRITA'S DISMAY, INDRA VANISHED.

BUT HE WAS NOT GOING TO GIVE UP.

I WILL CONTINUE WITH MY PENANCE AND WILL MAKE HIM APPEAR BEFORE ME AGAIN.

AT AMARAVATI —

IF I DON'T STOP HIM, HE WILL DESTROY HIM-SELF.

SO INDRA APPEARED ONCE MORE BEFORE YAVAKRITA.

YOUR METHOD IS BOUND TO FAIL. KNOW-LEDGE HAS TO BE ACQUIRED BY YEARS OF PATIENT STUDY UNDER THE GUID-ANCE OF A GURU.

BUT YAVAKRITA WAS ADAMANT.

O KING OF THE DEVAS, EITHER YOU GRANT MY DESIRE TOMORROW OR I CUT OFF MY LIMBS AND SACRIFICE THEM TO THE BLAZING FIRE.

IT IS SENSELESS TO ARGUE WITH HIM. I MUST FIND SOME OTHER WAY TO MAKE HIM UNDER-STAND.

HE'S VANISHED AGAIN!

EARLY NEXT MORNING, AS YAVAKRITA WENT TO THE SPOT ON THE BANK OF THE GANGA WHERE HE USUALLY PERFORMED HIS ABLUTIONS...

...A STRANGE SIGHT MET HIS EYES.

WHAT IS HE UP TO?

GOOD! HE HAS SEEN ME.

WHAT ARE YOU DOING?

PEOPLE WHO HAVE TO CROSS THE RIVER TO AND FRO MUST FIND THE JOURNEY VERY UNCOMFORTABLE.

I AM TRYING TO BRIDGE THE RIVER SO THAT THEY CAN EASILY WALK ACROSS.

31

YAVAKRITA BURST OUT LAUGHING.

SURELY YOU MUST KNOW THAT YOU CANNOT BRIDGE THAT MIGHTY RIVER WITH YOUR PUNY HANDFULS OF SAND. WHAT A FOOLISH PURSUIT!

IT'S NO LESS FOOLISH, MY GOOD MAN, THAN YOUR ATTEMPT TO ACQUIRE BY A FEW DAYS OR MONTHS OF PENANCES THAT WHICH TAKES YEARS OF PATIENT STUDY UNDER AN ABLE GURU!

SUDDENLY REALISING THAT IT WAS INDRA, YAVAKRITA FELL AT HIS FEET.

I HAVE UNDERSTOOD, MY LORD.

NALA DAMAYANTI

THE STEADFAST LOVERS

The route to your roots

NALA DAMAYANTI

King Nala's life is idyllic – until a cunning cousin tricks him out of his kingdom. Can the love of his beautiful Damayanti survive such a calamity? Will they be able to win back happiness? Full of twists and turns, the story of this ideal couple is told in the Mahabharata.

Script
Abid Surti

Illustrations
Souren Roy

Editor
Anant Pai

NALA DAMAYANTI

THOUSANDS OF YEARS AGO, NALA RULED OVER THE KINGDOM OF NISHADA. HE WAS GENEROUS AND NOBLE AND WAS LOVED BY HIS SUBJECTS. BUT HE WAS ALWAYS SAD. HIS FATHER HAD GONE TO A FOREST TO SPEND THE LAST YEARS OF HIS LIFE.

NALA'S COUSIN, PUSHKARA, ENVIED HIM HIS FAME.

NALA! I AM TIRED OF THE PEOPLE HERE AND HAVE DECIDED TO LEAVE.

NALA WAS LONELY AND WANDERED FROM PLACE TO PLACE. ONE DAY—

AH! I HAVE NEVER SEEN SUCH A BEAUTIFUL LAKE! NOR SUCH GRACEFUL SWANS!

WHY! THAT DAINTY SWAN HAS GOLDEN PLUMES!

SLOWLY AND SOFTLY HE CREPT FORWARD.

HE CAUGHT THE SWAN BY ITS LEG. THE BIRD CRIED OUT IN PAIN. THE OTHER SWANS LOOKED HELPLESSY ON.

DON'T BE AFRAID. I WON'T KILL YOU.

I SHALL KEEP YOU IN MY PALACE AND GIVE YOU PEARLS.

THE SWAN CONSOLED HIS WAILING MATES.

I HAVE TO GO WITH THE KING TO KEEP A PROMISE I MADE IN MY LAST BIRTH. I SHALL RETURN THE MOMENT MY WORK IS DONE.

NALA BROUGHT THE SWAN TO HIS PALACE. ONE DAY —

WHY ARE YOU WEEPING, O KING?

I HAVE BEEN AN UNHAPPY MAN FOR MANY MONTHS.

ONCE NARADA SPOKE TO ME ABOUT DAMAYANTI, THE CHARMING DAUGHTER OF KING BHEEMA OF KUNDANPUR. AND I DECIDED THEN AND THERE TO MARRY HER AND NO ONE ELSE.

4

IS THAT ALL THAT TROUBLES YOU? MAKE ARRANGEMENTS FOR THE WEDDING AND LEAVE THE REST TO ME. I'LL RETURN IN A WEEK.

THE SWAN FLEW AWAY INTO THE SKY...

... AND REACHED THE KINGDOM OF KUNDANPUR.

ENTERING THE ROYAL GARDEN, IT BEGAN CHANTING NALA'S NAME. DAMAYANTI LOOKED UP.

NALA!

NALA!

AH! WHAT A DEAR SWAN! IF ONLY I COULD HAVE IT!

AS DAMAYANTI WENT FORWARD TO CATCH THE SWAN, IT MOVED FARTHER AWAY.

AT LAST, WITH A SWIFT MOVEMENT, SHE CAUGHT IT.

YOU'VE BEEN REPEATING THE NAME 'NALA.' WHO IS HE?

THE SWAN SPOKE OF NALA AND PRAISED HIM HIGHLY.

KING NALA MUST BE A WONDERFUL MAN! I'LL MARRY HIM AND NONE OTHER.

THE SWAN RETURNED TO NALA.

I HAVE DONE MY JOB, O KING! DAMAYANTI WILL MARRY ONLY YOU.

I HAVE KEPT MY PROMISE. LET ME NOW GO BACK TO MY COMPANIONS.

I WILL MISS YOU, MY FRIEND, BUT I DON'T WANT TO KEEP YOU AWAY FROM YOUR FRIENDS.

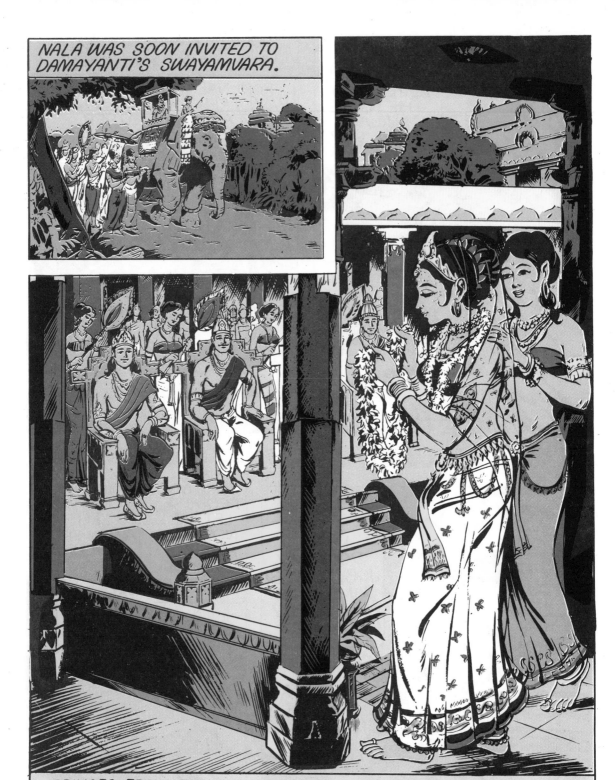

NALA WAS SOON INVITED TO DAMAYANTI'S SWAYAMVARA.

PRINCES FROM FAR AND NEAR HAD GATHERED IN THE SWAYAM-VARA HALL. DAMAYANTI ENTERED WITH THE GARLAND. THE PRINCES WERE RESTLESS. LITTLE DID THEY KNOW THAT DAMAYANTI'S GARLAND WAS MEANT ONLY FOR NALA.

DAMAYANTI GARLANDED NALA.

LONG LIVE KING NALA!

NALA BROUGHT DAMAYANTI TO HIS PALACE. PEOPLE, YOUNG AND OLD, DANCED WITH JOY.

HAPPY TIMES PASS QUICKLY. SOON, TWELVE YEARS WERE OVER. ONE DAY—

WHO ARE YOU?

DON'T YOU RE-MEMBER ME? I'M PUSHKARA, YOUR COUSIN.

9

I AM TIRED OF FOREST LIFE AND HAVE COME BACK TO ENJOY THE PLEASURES OF THE CITY ONCE AGAIN.

YOU ARE WELCOME HERE.

PUSHKARA, THIS PALACE IS BEING BUILT FOR YOU.

NALA TRIED HIS BEST TO KEEP HIS COUSIN HAPPY.

BEFORE LONG, EVEN HIS CROWN WILL BE MINE!

PUSHKARA WAS A CUNNING MAN.

PUSHKARA INVITED NALA TO GAMBLE WITH HIM NOW AND AGAIN.

BUT NALA KEPT ON LOSING.

NOW FOR THE LAST ROUND. THE WINNER GETS THE CROWN AND THE LOSER SPENDS THREE YEARS IN THE FOREST— AGREED?

AGREED!

THE DICE WERE CAST.

I HAVE WON! HA... HA...HA...! I'M THE RULER NOW!

NALA GAVE UP THE KINGDOM. DAMAYANTI SENT THE CHILDREN TO HER PARENTS AND WENT AWAY WITH NALA.

AS HE LEANED FORWARD, THE BIRDS FLEW AWAY WITH THE GARMENT—NALA'S ONLY BELONGING!

ONE DAY NALA NOTICED A FLOCK OF GOLDEN BIRDS...

...AND THREW HIS GARMENT OVER THE BIRDS TO TRAP THEM.

AT NIGHT THEY SLEPT ON THE BARE GROUND COVERED BY DAMAYANTI'S SARI.

EARLY NEXT MORNING, WHEN NALA WOKE UP, HE TORE A PIECE FROM DAMAYANTI'S SARI. WRAPPING HIMSELF IN IT, HE QUIETLY WALKED AWAY.

14

HE WALKED FOR A LONG TIME. SUDDENLY—

HELP!

HELP!

OH, HERE IS THE SERPENT GOD.

NALA JUMPED INTO THE FIRE.

A LITTLE LATER—

YOU'VE SAVED MY LIFE. I SHALL GIVE YOU SOMETHING IN RETURN.

WALK TEN STEPS.

OH! SERPENT GOD, WHAT HAVE YOU DONE?

I CHANGED YOUR FORM SO THAT YOU WON'T BE RECOGNISED. YOU'RE BAAHUK FROM TODAY.

KING RITUPARNA OF AYODHYA IS VERY GOOD AT THE GAME OF DICE. GO TO HIM IF YOU WISH TO KNOW THE SECRET OF THE GAME!

AND, PUT ON THIS MAGIC DRESS WHEN YOU WANT TO BECOME YOUR OLD SELF.

MEANWHILE DAMAYANTI WOKE UP.

WHERE HAS NALA GONE? WHY HAS HE LEFT ME ALONE IN THE FOREST?

NALA! OH, NALA!

DAMAYANTI WANDERED IN THE FOREST CRYING FOR NALA.

DAMAYANTI ASKED THE ANIMALS AND BIRDS.

O JUMPING DEER! O LITTLE SPARROW! HAVE YOU SEEN MY NALA?

A DEADLY PYTHON SAW DAMA-YANTI AND OPENED ITS JAWS.

IT CAUGHT DAMAYANTI'S LEG.

SUDDENLY A HUNTER'S ARROW
HIT AND KILLED THE PYTHON.

THEN —

WHO ARE YOU?
A GODDESS?
A HEAVENLY
DAMSEL?
MARRY ME!

OH, MY MISFORTUNE!
I WISH THE PYTHON
HAD KILLED ME...!
STAY WHERE YOU
ARE. IF YOU TAKE
ONE STEP FURTHER,
YOU WILL BE BURNT.

BY HER CURSE, THE HUNTER WAS BURNT TO ASHES.

STUMBLING AND FALLING, DAMA-YANTI REACHED THE RIVER BANK. THERE SHE MET A GROUP OF TRADERS.

OH TRADER, CAN YOU GIVE ME NEWS ABOUT NALA?

NALA? WHO'S HE?

AT NIGHT WHEN THE TRADERS WERE ASLEEP, A HERD OF ELEPHANTS CAME THAT WAY AND DESTROYED ALL THAT THEY CARRIED.

WE'VE LOST EVERYTHING! THIS WOMAN HAS BROUGHT US ILL LUCK.

BEAT HER!

BEAT HER!

DAMAYANTI RUNNING FOR HER LIFE, REACHED THE KINGDOM OF VIPRAPUR. CHILDREN TEASED HER AND CALLED HER MAD.

QUEEN BHANUMATI SAW HER FROM THE TERRACE.

SHE SEEMS TO BE A WOMAN FROM A GOOD FAMILY. CALL HER!

YOU ARE GOOD AT YOUR WORK.

SHE ENGAGED DAMAYANTI AS A MAID NOT KNOWING WHO SHE REALLY WAS

ONE DAY, THE MINISTER OF KUNDANPUR CAME TO VIPRAPUR.

ISN'T THAT QUEEN DAMAYANTI?

HOW DID YOU COME HERE?

I'VE BEEN SEARCHING A LONG TIME FOR YOU. I'LL TAKE YOU TO KUNDANPUR.

DAMAYANTI CAME TO KUNDANPUR. HER CHILDREN HAD GROWN UP. SHE WATCHED THEM AT PLAY AND MISSED NALA.

DAMAYANTI WAS STILL UNHAPPY.

HER FATHER CONSOLED HER.

ONE DAY, THE KING'S MINISTER SET OUT IN SEARCH OF NALA. SOON HE CAME TO AYODHYA.

AT KING RITUPARNA'S COURT, THE MINISTER SAID...

"A KING RAN AWAY. IN DUST THE JEWEL LAY. WHY HE RAN AWAY, THE JEWEL COULD NOT SAY."

A GOOD RIDDLE, INDEED! LET'S SEE WHO CAN SOLVE IT.

THE RIDDLE HAS GOT TO BE SOLVED!

EVERYONE WONDERED AT THE STRANGE WORDS OF THE MINISTER.

SUDDENLY—

MY LORD! PERMIT ME...

IT WAS NONE OTHER THAN NALA, WHO HAD ASSUMED THE NAME OF BAAHUK.

CAN A KING WITHOUT A CROWN, KEEP A JEWEL FOR HIS OWN?

BEAUTIFUL!

WELL DONE, BAAHUK!

EXCELLENT!

THE MINISTER RETURNED TO KUNDANPUR AND NARRATED THE EVENTS TO DAMAYANTI.

WHO CARES IF HE IS UGLY AND DEFORMED... I AM SURE, HE IS NALA.

IN THAT CASE WE'LL CALL HIM HERE AND FIND OUT.

24

THE MINISTER AGAIN WENT TO AYODHYA.
MY LORD! DAMAYANTI HAS AGREED TO REMARRY.
OH, GOD! COULD THIS BE TRUE?

By the time they reached Kundanpur, they had exchanged their secrets.

MEANWHILE, BAAHUK SAW HIS TWO CHILDREN FROM THE TERRACE.

DAMAYANTI OBSERVED THIS FROM THE PALACE. SHE CAME RUNNING TO MEET HIM.

I'M SURE YOU ARE NALA! HOW CAN I THANK YOU FOR COMING!

HE RAN UP TO THEM AND HUGGED THEM.

BUT WERE YOU GOING TO MARRY AGAIN, DAMAYANTI?

NO. IT WAS A TRICK TO GET YOU HERE. WHO ELSE BUT YOU COULD TRAVEL SUCH A LONG DISTANCE IN ONE DAY?

NALA PUT ON THE MAGIC DRESS AND —

SEEING NALA SAFE AND SOUND, THE PEOPLE WENT CRAZY WITH JOY.

NALA RETURNED TO HIS PALACE WITH DAMAYANTI AND THE CHILDREN.

PUSHKARA! I HAVE SPENT MY THREE YEARS IN THE FOREST. COME, LET'S HAVE AN-OTHER GAME OF DICE.

VERY WELL! THE WINNER WILL HAVE THE KINGDOM. AND THE LOSER WILL GO TO THE FOREST.

THEY SETTLED DOWN TO THE GAME. NALA HAD MASTERED THE GAME OF DICE WITH THE HELP OF KING RITUPARNA. IT WAS PUSHKARA'S TURN TO LOSE.

AND HE DID.

PUSHKARA! I'VE WON! I'VE WON!

BUT, I WON'T SEND YOU TO THE FOREST. YOU MAY CONTINUE TO LIVE HERE!

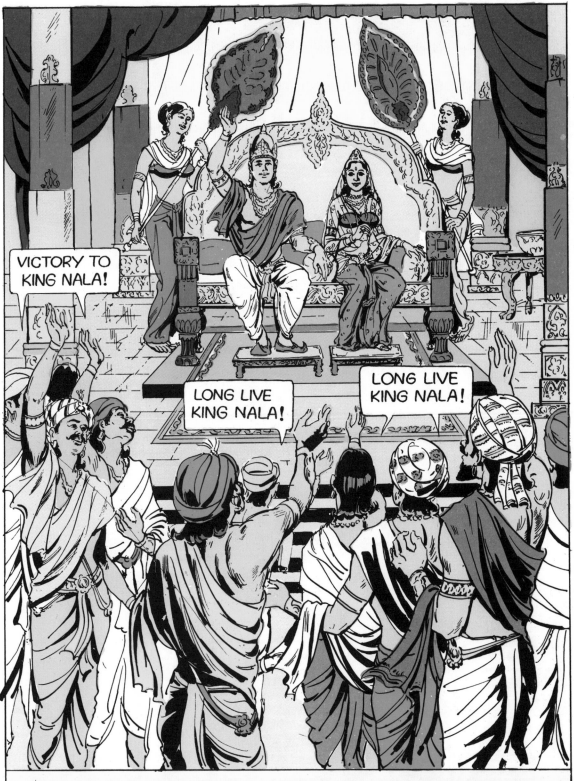

ONCE AGAIN, NALA WORE THE CROWN. DAMAYANTI WAS HIS QUEEN.
THEY LIVED HAPPILY FOR MANY YEARS AND RULED THE COUNTRY WELL.

Suppandi and his friends are all packed!

time your favourite characters are bringing their (mis)adventures to your holiday. Media introduces its special travel collection of Tinkle Digests, Amar Chitra ha comics and Karadi Tales picture books (for the younger globetrotters), to make travels more fun.

www.amarchitrakatha.com

Make sure you're packed. Log on to our website now to buy any comic or picture book with your special 25%* discount code: 'NGT 25', and have your favourite travel companions delivered straight to your doorstep.

KACHA AND DEVAYANI

STAR-CROSSED LOVERS

www.amarchitrakatha.com

The route to your roots

KACHA AND DEVAYANI

While the war was raging between the devas and asuras, the devas sent Kacha to the preceptor of the asuras. Kacha approached the asura guru as a student. It was in this background of hate, war and rivalry that the beautiful Devayani, the proud daughter, of the asura guru, fell in love with Kacha, the man who was being watched by the asuras with increasing suspicion – they knew Kacha was seeking the key to immortality from their guru. Then a twist in the tale throws the dreams of the young couple into disarray.

Script
Kamala Chandrakant

Illustrations
Souren Roy

Editor
Anant Pai

Cover illustration by: Dayal Patkar

KACHA DEVAYANI

IN THE DAYS OF YORE, THE DEVAS AND THE ASURAS WERE EVER
STRUGGLING FOR THE LORDSHIP OF THE THREE WORLDS.

BOTH HAD WISE MEN TO GUIDE THEM. BRIHASPATI, THE SON OF SAGE ANGIRAS, LIVED IN THE ABODE OF INDRA, KING OF THE DEVAS.

AND SHUKRACHARYA THE FAVOURITE PUPIL OF SAGE ANGIRAS, LIVED IN THE CAPITAL CITY OF THE ASURA KING, VRISHAPARVA.

BUT OF THE TWO, SHUKRACHARYA ALONE KNEW THE CRAFT OF SANJIVANI, THE SECRET OF REVIVING THE DEAD.

AS LONG AS SHUKRACHARYA IS WITH US, OUR NUMBERS SHALL NEVER DECREASE.

HEAR!

HEAR!

HEAR!

FOR, THOSE WHO HAD FALLEN IN BATTLE WERE SIMPLY BROUGHT BACK TO LIFE, TO CONTINUE THE WAR ON THE DEVAS.

THE VALIANT DEVAS, TIRED OF THE UNEQUAL STRUGGLE WENT TO THE BRILLIANT, HANDSOME YOUTH, KACHA, THE SON OF BRIHASPATI.

YOU MUST GO TO SHUKRACHARYA AND LEARN THE CRAFT OF SANJIVANI. ONLY THEN CAN WE VANQUISH OUR SWORN ENEMIES.

THE OBEDIENT AND DUTIFUL KACHA IMMEDIATELY SET OUT TO MEET SHUKRACHARYA.

I WONDER WHAT AWAITS ME IN THE CAPITAL CITY OF THE ASURAS.

THERE HE HUMBLY PRESENTED HIMSELF BEFORE THE GREAT WISE ONE.

I AM KACHA, THE SON OF BRIHASPATI. I WISH TO BECOME YOUR DISCIPLE. I SHALL OBEY YOU AND SERVE YOU LOYALLY.

SHUKRACHARYA GAVE HIM A WARM WELCOME.

I ACCEPT YOU AS MY PUPIL, O WORTHY KACHA, SON OF LEARNED BRIHASPATI.

SHUKRACHARYA HAD A DAUGHTER, DEVAYANI, WHOM HE LOVED DEARLY.

COME DEVAYANI, MY CHILD. MEET THE WORTHY KACHA, WHO HAS VOWED TO BE MY PUPIL TILL THE PERIOD OF HIS STUDIES IS OVER.

ALL LEARNING IN THOSE DAYS WAS HANDED DOWN BY WORD OF MOUTH. THE PUPIL LIVED WITH HIS GURU'S FAMILY AS ONE OF HIS HOUSEHOLD. IN RETURN FOR HIS EDUCATION, HE SERVED HIS GURU WITH LOVE AND DEVOTION.

SO KACHA HELPED DEVAYANI WITH HER DAILY CHORES.

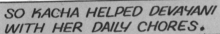

LET ME DRAW THE WATER FOR YOU.

AND TENDERLY FULFILLED HER SLIGHTEST WISH.

HERE, DEVAYANI! I PICKED THEM FOR YOU.

WITHIN A FEW DAYS OF HIS ARRIVAL, KACHA FOUND HIMSELF SPENDING ALL HIS LEISURE HOURS IN THE COMPANY OF THE LIVELY DEVAYANI.

MUSIC, SONG AND DANCE NEVER FAIL TO GIVE ME PLEASURE. DO ANY OF THESE ARTS INTEREST YOU?

I CAN SING, DANCE AND PLAY ANY INSTRUMENT.

HOW WELL HE SINGS! HOW PEACEFUL IS HIS EXPRESSION! AND HOW IT DOES FILL MY HEART WITH A YEARNING, I DON'T UNDERSTAND!

AND KACHA WON HIS WAY INTO DEVAYANI'S HEART.

WHERE COULD HE BE? HAS HE TIRED OF MY COMPANY? HAVE I DONE ANYTHING TO OFFEND HIM?

BUT DEVAYANI COULD NOT EVEN PRETEND TO BE ANGRY FOR LONG.

COME, LET US GO TO OUR FAVOURITE BOWER.

IT IS NOT AS WARM IN THE LAND OF DEVAS AS IT IS HERE.

WHERE IS KACHA? IT IS TIME...

I SHALL CALL HIM. HE IS WITH THE CATTLE

AND SO KACHA LIVED AND LEARNED IN THE HOME OF HIS GURU.

BUT AS THE YEARS PASSED, THE ASURAS BECAME SUSPICIOUS OF KACHA.

IT IS STRANGE! WHY SHOULD THE SON OF THE LEARNED BRIHASPATI COME TO OUR CITY AND CHOOSE SHUKRA-CHARYA FOR HIS GURU?

I SENSE TREACHERY. THE ONLY KNOWLEDGE SHUKRACHARYA HAS, THAT KACHA'S FATHER HAS NOT, IS THE SECRET CRAFT OF SANJIVANI.

ALL THE ASURAS ROSE AS ONE ROARING ANGRILY.

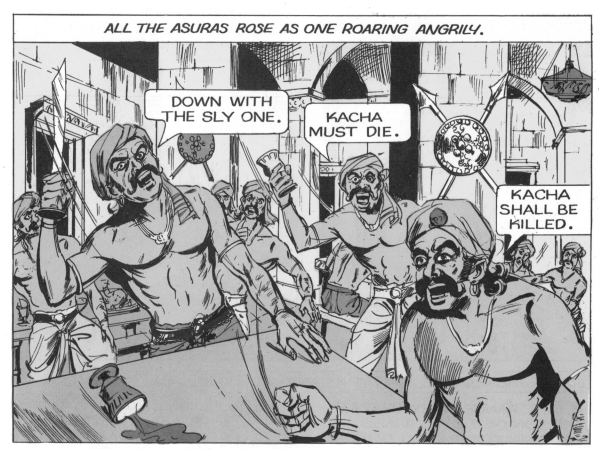

DOWN WITH THE SLY ONE.

KACHA MUST DIE.

KACHA SHALL BE KILLED.

WAIT! PATIENCE! WE SHALL HAVE TO DO THIS IN SECRECY. A GURU WILL NOT LET HIS PUPIL BE SLAIN.

THE ASURAS WAITED, BUT IMPATIENTLY. THEN ONE DAY...

THE ASURAS FELL UPON HIM AND SLEW HIM.

THEY CUT HIM INTO PIECES.

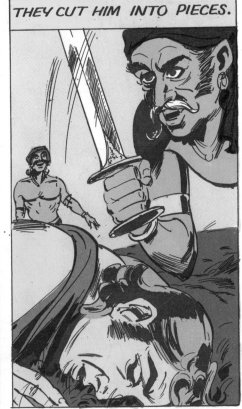

AND FED HIS FLESH TO THEIR DOGS.

HA!

HA!

AS USUAL DEVAYANI WAITED FOR HIM.

IT IS LATE! THE CATTLE HAVE NOT RETURNED AND NEITHER HAS HE.

THERE THEY COME! BUT WHY DO THEY RETURN WITHOUT KACHA? A NAMELESS FEAR GRIPS ME.

IT IS LATE AND YOUR PRAYERS ARE OVER. THE CATTLE HAVE COME HOME WITHOUT KACHA. IF HE IS DEAD, I DO NOT WANT TO LIVE ANY MORE

DO NOT WEEP, MY CHILD. WILL NOT YOUR FATHER, WHO HAS REVIVED COUNTLESS ASURA WARRIORS, USE HIS SECRET FOR HIS OWN DAUGHTER'S HAPPINESS?

SHUKRACHARYA CLOSED HIS EYES AND LO!

KACHA STOOD BEFORE DEVAYANI.

WHERE DID YOU VANISH? WHY DID YOU TEASE ME SO?

THE ASURAS KILLED ME! I DO NOT KNOW HOW I CAME BACK TO LIFE BUT HERE I AM.

KACHA CONTINUED LIVING IN THE HOME OF HIS GURU. ONE DAY –

LONG AGO, WHILE WALKING DEEP IN THE FOREST WITH MY FATHER, I HAD SEEN SOME FLOWERS. THEIR PERFUME STILL LINGERS IN MY MEMORY. KACHA, WILL YOU BRING SOME FOR ME? THEY BLOOM ONLY IN THIS SEASON.

KACHA COULD HARDLY REFUSE THE ENCHANTING DEVAYANI SUCH A REQUEST.

SO HE WANDERED DEEP INTO THE FOREST IN SEARCH OF THE FLOWERS. THE ASURAS WERE WAITING FOR JUST SUCH AN OPPORTUNITY.

THEY WAYLAID HIM AND SLEW HIM.

THIS TIME THEY CARRIED HIS BODY TO A LONELY SPOT. THERE –

WE SHALL POUND HIS CARCASS INTO PASTE AND DISSOLVE IT IN THE WATERS OF THE OCEAN.

HOURS LATER AT SHUKRACHARYA'S HOME —

KACHA IS AWAY LONG ENOUGH TO COLLECT FLOWERS FOR TEN MAIDENS. I WONDER WHAT KEEPS HIM?

WHY SHOULD I WORRY? I HAVE ONLY TO TELL FATHER AND KACHA WITH MY FLOWERS WILL STAND BEFORE ME.

MEANWHILE —

I WONDER WHAT KEEPS KACHA. IT IS TIME FOR HIS STUDIES. AND HE IS PROMPT. FOR SOME REASON THE ASURAS WISH TO KILL MY DISCIPLE. I FEAR HE IS IN THEIR CLUTCHES ONCE AGAIN.

DEVAYANI APPROACHED SHUKRACHARYA AND HIS SUSPICIONS WERE CONFIRMED.

FATHER!

DO NOT BE UPSET, MY CHILD.

ONCE AGAIN HE USED HIS SECRET KNOWLEDGE TO RECALL KACHA.

I HAVE BAD NEWS FOR YOU! KACHA LIVES.

THE ASURAS WERE AT THEIR WIT'S END.

HOW CAN WE KILL KACHA IF SHUKRACHARYA KEEPS BRINGING HIM BACK TO LIFE?

AT LAST ONE OF THEM HAD AN IDEA.

THE NEXT EVENING WHEN KACHA WAS DRIVING THE CATTLE HOME AS USUAL—

HIS BODY WAS CREMATED.

THE ASHES WERE CAREFULLY COLLECTED...

... AND MIXED INTO A GOBLET OF WINE.

THE GREYING ASURA THEN TOOK THE GOBLET OF WINE TO SHUKRACHARYA.

O WISE ONE! WE BRING YOU THIS HUMBLE GIFT IN GRATITUDE FOR KEEPING OUR NUMBERS CONSTANT.

IF SHUKRACHARYA HAD A WEAKNESS IT WAS FOR WINE. HE EMPTIED THE CONTENTS OF THE GOBLET IN ONE GULP.

LONG LIVE THE ASURAS!

OH KACHA!
HOW MANY MORE
DEATHS WILL YOU
HAVE TO DIE
BEFORE THE ASURAS
LEAVE YOU ALONE?
WILL YOU EVER
BE MINE?

THE CATTLE RETURNED HOME ONCE MORE WITHOUT KACHA.

FATHER!
WITHOUT KACHA
I AM AS GOOD AS
DEAD. PLEASE
BRING HIM BACK
TO LIFE.

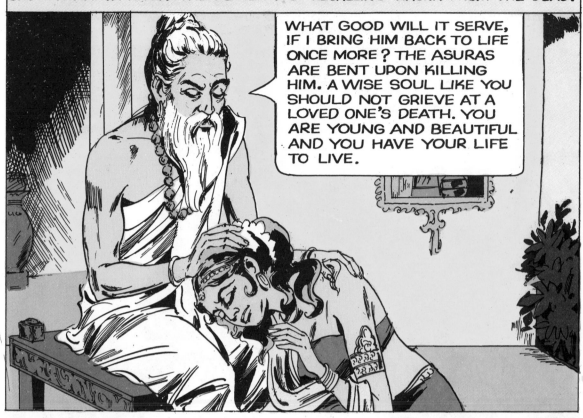

WHAT GOOD WILL IT SERVE, IF I BRING HIM BACK TO LIFE ONCE MORE? THE ASURAS ARE BENT UPON KILLING HIM. A WISE SOUL LIKE YOU SHOULD NOT GRIEVE AT A LOVED ONE'S DEATH. YOU ARE YOUNG AND BEAUTIFUL AND YOU HAVE YOUR LIFE TO LIVE.

BUT DEVAYANI'S LOVE FOR KACHA KNEW NO REASONING.

KACHA WAS A GOOD PUPIL AND LOYAL TO US. I LOVED HIM DEARLY AND NOW THAT HE IS DEAD, I DO NOT WISH TO LIVE.

PLEASE, FATHER, I DON'T WANT TO EAT ANYTHING.

I CAN'T BEAR YOUR SORROW.

HENCEFORTH WINE SHALL BE FORBIDDEN FOR THOSE ENGAGED IN THE PURSUIT OF WISDOM.

KACHA CAN COME OUT ONLY BY KILLING ME.

BUT FATHER, I WILL NOT LIVE IF EITHER OF YOU DIES.

AS SHUKRACHARYA THOUGHT OF A WAY OUT, THE REAL PURPOSE OF KACHA'S VISIT DAWNED UPON HIM.

I NOW SEE WHY YOU CAME AND TRULY YOU HAVE SUCCEEDED. THERE IS ONLY ONE WAY BY WHICH BOTH OF US CAN SURVIVE TO ENSURE DEVAYANI'S HAPPINESS. I WILL HAVE TO TEACH YOU THE CRAFT OF SANJIVANI.

AND SO KACHA LEARNED THE CRAFT FOR WHICH HE HAD COME TO THE HOUSE OF SHUKRACHARYA IN THE CITY OF THE ASURAS AND EMERGED FROM SHUKRACHARYA'S MANGLED BODY.

HE IMMEDIATELY BROUGHT HIS GURU BACK TO LIFE.

SHUKRACHARYA COULD NOT HELP BEING PLEASED WITH HIS PUPIL'S WISDOM.

SHUKRACHARYA THEN WENT TO SEE THE ASURAS.

YOU FOOLS! KACHA NOW KNOWS MY SECRET CRAFT. YOU HELPED HIM LEARN IT.

BUT REST ASSURED. HE WILL CONTINUE TO LIVE WITH ME FOR THE FAULTLESS DEVAYANI LOVES HIM.

BUT KACHA WAS ONLY WAITING FOR THE FORMAL PERIOD OF HIS STUDIES TO COME TO AN END.

HOW WILL I BREAK THE NEWS TO DEVAYANI? SHE WILL BE HEART-BROKEN. BUT I MUST FULFIL MY DUTIES.

AT LAST THE DAY ARRIVED WHEN KACHA COULD LEAVE.

MY DAYS OF LIVING WITH MY GURU ARE OVER. I HAVE TO RETURN TO MY PEOPLE. MAY I TAKE MY LEAVE WITH YOUR BLESSING?

DOES DEVAYANI KNOW OF HIS DECISION? I WONDER!

NEXT KACHA WENT TO DEVAYANI. SHE WAS FONDLING A DEER IN HER GARDEN.

DEVAYANI!

I KNEW HE WOULD COME. FROM TO-DAY HE IS FREE TO MARRY. HIS PERIOD OF LEARNING IS OVER. HE MAY NOW BECOME A HOUSEHOLDER

BUT DEVAYANI'S SMILES WERE SOON TO DISSOLVE INTO TEARS.

DEVAYANI, I HAVE COME TO TAKE MY LEAVE OF YOU. MY PERIOD OF STUDIES IS OVER AND I MUST RETURN TO MY PEOPLE TO FULFIL MY DUTIES.

NOBLE KACHA! WHILE YOU WERE A STUDENT, I LOVED YOU, BUT COULD NOT SPEAK OUT. NOW THAT YOU ARE FREE TO MARRY WILL YOU NOT TAKE ME FOR YOUR WIFE?

DON'T YOU REMEMBER THE HAPPY DAYS WE HAVE SHARED? WHY DO YOU STAND ALOOF? HAVE I WRONGED YOU IN ANY WAY?

KACHA HELD DEVAYANI'S HAND TENDERLY.

PEERLESS ONE! I WAS REBORN IN YOUR FATHER'S STOMACH. I AM THEREFORE YOUR BROTHER. I CAN'T MARRY YOU. I MUST RETURN.

YOU MADE USE OF ONE WHO WAS SINLESS IN HER DEVOTION TO YOU.

I THEREFORE LAY A CURSE ON YOU. YOU WILL NEVER BE ABLE TO USE THE CRAFT OF SANJIVANI.

DEAREST DEVAYANI, IT IS WRONG OF YOU TO CURSE ME. FOR THIS, NO RISHI'S SON WILL EVER MARRY YOU. BUT I MAY STILL TEACH THE CRAFT OF SANJIVANI TO OTHERS.

THEN KACHA DEPARTED FOR THE ABODE OF INDRA, KING OF THE DEVAS.

WITH THE PASSAGE OF TIME, DEVAYANI COMPLETELY FORGOT ABOUT THE EXISTENCE OF KACHA.

MAY I JOIN SHARMISHTHA AND THE OTHERS AT THE POOL?

CERTAINLY! YOU MAY, MY CHILD! BUT BE CAREFUL.

INDRA AND SHACHI

THE LORD OF HEAVEN AND HIS DEVOTED WIFE

www.amarchitrakatha.com

The route to your roots

INDRA AND
SHACHI

Even gods can be prey to their inner torments. Lying and killing for the sake of peace and order, Indra felt he was unworthy of being king of heaven. A new king was installed on his throne! Now it was up to Indra's wife Shachi to ensure that his honour survived. Would the gods ever regain their respect for her beloved?

Script
Lakshmi Seshadri

Illustrations
M.N.Nangare

Editor
Anant Pai

INDRA AND SHACHI

INDRA WAS THE KING OF THE DEVAS. HE LIVED WITH HIS QUEEN, SHACHI IN HIS CELESTIAL CITY, AMARAVATI.

LORD! WE ARE SO HAPPY THAT I FEAR IT MIGHT NOT LAST.

NOTHING UNTOWARD CAN HAPPEN TO US, MY DEAR.

BUT THERE WAS CAUSE FOR THEM TO FEAR. AT THAT VERY MOMENT A SON WAS BORN TO TVASHTA, INDRA'S ENEMY.

MY SON, YOU SHALL BECOME KING OF THE GODS.

YOU SHALL RECITE THE VEDAS WITH ONE HEAD...

...CONSUME THE DIVINE SURA WITH THE OTHER AND...

...WATCH THE WORLD WITH THE THIRD.

TRISHIRAS GREW UP FAST. HE BECAME STRONG-WILLED AND POWERFUL.

I SHALL PERFORM SEVERE PENANCES AND DESTROY INDRA, MY FATHER'S ENEMY.

INDRA HEARD OF TRISHIRAS AND OF HIS INTENSE PENANCE TO DESTROY HIM. HE SENT FOR THE APSARAS, THE CELESTIAL MAIDENS...

YOU MUST DISTRACT TRISHIRAS AND BREAK HIS PENANCE.

WE WILL LEAD HIM AWAY FROM MEDITATION INTO A LIFE OF PLEASURE.

THE APSARAS PREPARED THEMSELVES.

WE WILL TEMPT HIM WITH THESE FRUITS AND FLOWERS.

I WILL DANCE.

YOUR VOICE IS SWEET AND ENCHANTING. YOU MUST SING.

THEIR CHARMS WERE HEAVENLY. BUT TRISHIRAS WAS UNMOVED.

3

THE APSARAS RETURNED TO INDRA.

WE HAVE FAILED. TRISHIRAS IS STEADFAST...

AT THIS RATE HE WILL USURP MY THRONE. I MUST KILL HIM.

SHACHI WAS WORRIED.

BE CAREFUL! I FEAR FOR YOUR SAFETY.

INDRA THREW HIS THUNDERBOLT AT TRISHIRAS WHILE HE WAS PRAYING.

TRISHIRAS FELL DEAD BUT HIS EYES REMAINED UNSHUT AND STARING.

THOSE EYES HAUNT ME.

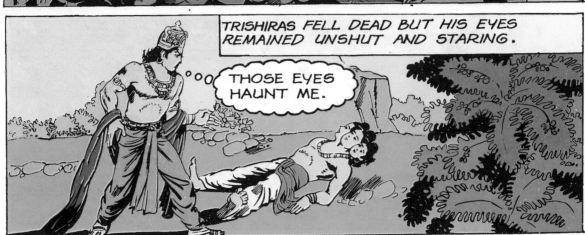

4

I MUST GET THEM CLOSED.

THEY DRAIN ME OF ALL MY STRENGTH.

AT THAT MOMENT A WOODCUTTER HAPPENED TO PASS BY.

PLEASE CUT HIS HEADS OFF WITH YOUR AXE.

HIS NECK IS TOO THICK. MY AXE WILL BECOME BLUNT.

MY THUNDER-BOLT SHALL GIVE IT AN EDGE, FINE AND STRONG.

THE WOODCUTTER CUT TRISHIRAS' HEADS OFF.

NOW I WILL HAVE TO ATONE FOR MY SIN. I HAVE MURDERED A BRAHMAN.

INDRA DID PENANCE FOR A LONG TIME.

FINALLY, A DIVINE VOICE SPOKE TO HIM.

ARISE, INDRA. YOU HAVE ATONED FOR YOUR SIN BY YOUR PENANCE.

NOW I AM FREE. I SHALL RETURN TO AMARAVATI.

I HAVE COME HOME VICTORIOUS.

THANKS BE TO GOD.

MEANWHILE TVASHTA HEARD OF TRISHIRAS' DEATH. HE WAS DEEPLY GRIEVED AND VERY ANGRY.

I SHALL AVENGE MY SON'S DEATH. FROM THE POWER OF MY PRAYERS...

...SHALL RISE AN ASURA.

TVASHTA PERFORMED A SACRIFICE AND CREATED AN ASURA.

YOU ARE VRITRA. GO FORTH AND KILL INDRA.

WHEN INDRA HEARD OF VRITRA, HE PREPARED TO MEET THE CHALLENGE.

VRITRA HAS COME TO AVENGE TRISHIRAS.

I KNEW NO GOOD WOULD COME OF KILLING TRISHIRAS.

THERE WAS A TERRIBLE BATTLE IN WHICH VRITRA CAUGHT INDRA BETWEEN HIS TEETH.

HE HAS CAUGHT INDRA.

QUICK! HAND ME THE *JRIMBHAKA ASTRA.

THE JRIMBHAKA ASTRA FOUND ITS MARK.

I CANNOT CONTROL THESE YAWNS. THAT ASTRA DOES IT.

THIS IS THE MOMENT FOR ME.

VRITRA YAWNED...

INDRA MADE HIMSELF TINY AND ESCAPED.

* AN ARROW WHICH MAKES A MAN YAWN.

8

HE AND HIS SUBJECTS WENT TO VISHNU FOR ADVICE.

LORD, HELP US.

MAKE PEACE WITH VRITRA. THEN WATCH FOR YOUR CHANCE TO KILL HIM. I WILL HELP YOU.

INDRA MADE PEACE WITH VRITRA. BUT VRITRA WAS WARY.

LET US BE FRIENDS! I ADMIRE YOU!

ALL RIGHT. BUT ON MY CONDITIONS.

YOU MUST NOT KILL ME WITH ANY WEAPON— WET OR DRY, OF WOOD OR OF STONE...

...BY DAY OR BY NIGHT!

I AGREE.

ONE EVENING THEY WERE ON THE SEA-SHORE.

I MUST KILL HIM SOON —BUT WITHOUT USING A WEAPON.

FOAM CANNOT BE CONSIDERED A WEAPON. VISHNU HAS PROMISED TO HELP ME.

THIS TWILIGHT IS NEITHER NIGHT NOR DAY. FOAM IS NEITHER WET NOR DRY. VISHNU, HELP ME!

VISHNU ENTERED THE FOAM AND WHEN INDRA THREW IT AT VRITRA, HE WAS KILLED IMMEDIATELY BY THE POWER OF VISHNU WITHIN IT.

BUT AS INDRA HAD BETRAYED VRITRA HE WAS ASHAMED TO FACE THE WORLD.

I HAVE KILLED VRITRA. BUT I CANNOT SHOW MY FACE TO ANYONE.

I SHALL HIDE WHERE NONE CAN FIND ME.

INDRA RAN AWAY. ALL WAS DARKNESS AND CHAOS, ON EARTH AND IN HEAVEN.

THERE IS NO LIGHT ANYWHERE.

OH! SOMEONE IS BEATING ME IN THE DARK.

HOW DARE YOU ENTER MY HOUSE?

THE DEVAS MET IN A COUNCIL.

WITHOUT A KING THE HEAVENS ARE IN CHAOS.

WE CANNOT ALLOW THIS ANARCHY TO GO ON.

INDRA HAS DESERTED US.

WE MUST FIND ANOTHER KING.

KING NAHUSHA IS A GOOD AND PIOUS MAN. SHALL WE SELECT HIM?

YES! YES!

LET US GO TO EARTH AND INVITE HIM TO BE OUR KING.

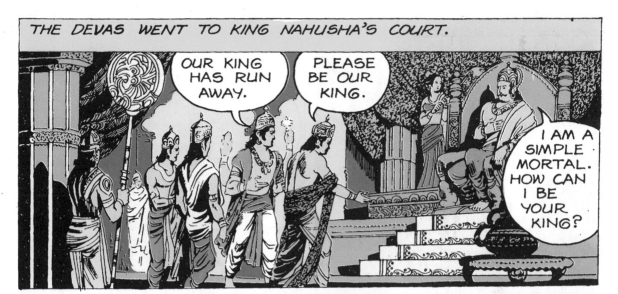

OUR KING HAS RUN AWAY.

PLEASE BE OUR KING.

I AM A SIMPLE MORTAL. HOW CAN I BE YOUR KING?

WE WILL INVEST YOU WITH OUR POWERS AND STRENGTH.

THERE IS NO ONE ELSE. YOU MUST AGREE!

WELL. IF YOU INSIST.

THE DEVAS MADE NAHUSHA THEIR KING.

ISN'T THIS INDRA'S FAMOUS ELEPHANT? MAY I RIDE ON IT?

THIS KALPATARU IS YOURS. IT WILL GIVE YOU WHATEVER YOU WISH FOR.

I AM A LUCKY MAN TO OWN THIS.

THIS IS YOUR PALACE ND GARDEN. YOU MAY GIVE YOUR ORDERS. WE ARE HERE TO OBEY THEM.

YOU ARE ALL SO KIND. I DO NOT DESERVE ALL THIS.

WHO IS THAT BEING WHO GOES PAST WITHOUT BOWING TO HIS KING? BRING HIM HERE!

HEY, YOU SAGE THERE! COMPOSE A VERSE IN PRAISE OF ME.

IT IS HOT! LET ONE OF THE *MARUTS BLOW COOL BREEZE ON ME.

THE DEVAS WERE VERY UNHAPPY.

HE ORDERS US ABOUT AS IF WE WERE HIS SLAVES!

HE IS UNBEARABLE.

BE CAREFUL! HE MAY HEAR US!

* THE GODS OF WIND.

WHO IS THAT!

ONE DAY NAHUSHA SAW SHACHI IN THE PARK.

OUR QUEEN, SHACHI DEVI.

AS I AM THE KING HERE, SHE IS MY QUEEN.

GO AT ONCE AND BRING HER HERE!

DON'T DO THAT! SHE IS DEVOTED TO INDRA.

TERRIFIED, SHACHI RAN TO THE HOUSE OF BRIHASPATI, THE GURU OF THE DEVAS.

REVERED ONE, YOU KNOW I AM INDRA'S DEVOTED WIFE. SAVE ME FROM NAHUSHA.

DO NOT WORRY. YOU ARE SAFE HERE.

NAHUSHA WAS VERY ANGRY WHEN HE HEARD THAT SHACHI WAS IN BRIHASPATI'S HOUSE.

GO AT ONCE AND BRING HER HERE.

YES, SIR.

THE DEVAS TREMBLED BEFORE NAHUSHA'S FURY. THEY RAN TO BRIHASPATI'S HOUSE.

YOU MUST SEND OUR QUEEN, SHACHI TO NAHUSHA. OTHERWISE HE WILL DESTROY AMARAVATI IN ANGER.

SHE IS UNDER MY CARE. I WILL NOT FORCE HER TO GO WITH YOU.

WE CANNOT GO BACK WITHOUT HER. MAY WE AT LEAST SPEAK TO HER?

CERTAINLY! SHE WILL SPEAK TO YOU.

SHACHI CAME OUT AND MET THEM.

O GRACIOUS QUEEN, HELP US! TALK TO NAHUSHA.

GO WITH THEM SHACHI. ASK NAHUSHA TO GRANT YOU SOME TIME. MEANWHILE WE SHALL THINK OF A PLAN TO SAVE YOU FROM HIM.

SO, PROMPTED BY BRIHASPATI, SHACHI WENT WITH THE DEVAS TO NAHUSHA.

FIRST LET US SEARCH FOR MY LORD. IF HE CANNOT BE FOUND I SHALL BECOME YOUR QUEEN.

THAT IS REASONABLE. I AGREE.

THE DEVAS THEN WENT TO VISHNU FOR ADVICE.

WE MUST RESCUE OUR QUEEN. TELL US WHAT WE SHOULD DO NOW!

FIND OUT INDRA AND MAKE HIM PERFORM AN ASHWAMEDHA TO ATONE FOR THE SIN OF KILLING VRITRA, BY DECEIT.

AGNI, THE FIRE-GOD, LED THE SEARCH FOR INDRA.

COME ON! WE WILL FIND HIM SOMEHOW.

YES, HE MUST BE FOUND.

AT LAST THEY FOUND INDRA.

YOU MUST PERFORM THE ASHWAMEDHA TO ATONE FOR YOUR SIN.

THEN YOU MUST COME AND ATTACK NAHUSHA.

INDRA PERFORMED THE ASHWAMEDHA...

...AND THEN SET OUT TO CHALLENGE NAHUSHA.

I DO NOT FEEL DESOLATE ANY MORE.

COME AND DRIVE OUT NAHUSHA.

SHACHI HEARD THAT INDRA WAS COMING.

MAY HE DEFEAT NAHUSHA.

SO DID NAHUSHA.

I MUST GET INDRA OUT OF MY WAY.

INDRA CONFRONTED NAHUSHA.

HE IS TOO POWERFUL. I CANNOT FACE HIM.

THIS WEAKLING? IS THIS THE MIGHTY INDRA?

INDRA RAN AWAY.

WHY DO I QUAKE IN FEAR?

SHACHI WEPT.

I WOULD GIVE MY LIFE TO HELP HIM.

SHACHI PRAYED TO UPASHRUTI, A GODDESS OF THE NIGHT.

OH MIGHTY GODDESS! HELP ME!

UPASHRUTI APPEARED BEFORE SHACHI.

WHAT CAN I DO FOR YOU, MY CHILD?

MOTHER! TAKE ME TO MY LORD.

22

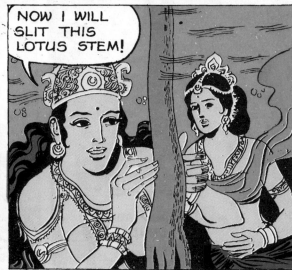

24

UPASHRUTI SLIT THE STEM. INSIDE COWERED A TINY INDRA.

HOW CAN I GET IN THERE AND SPEAK TO HIM?

I WILL MAKE YOU TINY LIKE HIM.

WHY DID YOU COME HERE?

LORD! YOU DO NOT KNOW MY PLIGHT.

AFTER SHACHI HAD EXPLAINED THE WHOLE SITUATION—

YOU MUST SAVE ME, OR NAHUSHA WILL MAKE ME HIS QUEEN TOMORROW.

INDRA TOLD HER WHAT SHE SHOULD DO.

GO QUICKLY AND DO AS I HAVE TOLD YOU.

I HOPE WE SUCCEED.

I HAVE FINISHED. LET US GO BACK.

THE NEXT MORNING SHACHI WENT TO NAHUSHA.

INDRA HAS RUN AWAY. I AM READY TO BE YOUR QUEEN.

I EXPECTED THIS.

INDRA USED TO COME TO MY PALACE...

"...SOMETIMES ON HIS WHITE ELEPHANT..."

"...SOMETIMES ON A HORSE..."

"...SOMETIMES IN HIS CHARIOT."

I HAVE A SPECIAL REQUEST TO MAKE. YOU SHOULD COME TO ME IN A PALANQUIN BORNE BY THE SEVEN SAGES.

THAT IS EASY. I AM THEIR KING. I WILL COME THIS EVENING.

TELL THE SEVEN SAGES TO BE READY TO CARRY MY PALANQUIN.

I SHALL PUT ON MY FINEST CLOTHES AND JEWELS.

NAHUSHA SET OUT IN THE PALANQUIN BORNE BY THE SEVEN SAGES.

28

MEANWHILE SHACHI WENT TO BRIHASPATI'S HOUSE.

I HAVE DONE MY PART.

THEN I SHALL SEND FOR INDRA.

BRIHASPATI INVOKED AGNI IN A SACRIFICE.

AGNI! YOU MUST FIND INDRA AND BRING HIM HERE, AT ONCE.

I WILL DO MY BEST. THE MARUTS WILL HELP ME MOVE QUICKLY.

AGNI CALLED THE DEVAS.

THE TIME HAS COME TO FORCE INDRA TO COME HERE.

WE WILL FOLLOW AS QUICKLY AS WE CAN.

WE WILL BLOW YOU AHEAD. THE OTHERS CAN FOLLOW.

AT THAT MOMENT NAHUSHA WAS ON HIS WAY TO SHACHI'S PALACE.

LAZY FELLOWS! HOW SLOW THEY ARE!

IT IS ALL THE FAULT OF AGASTYA. BECAUSE HE IS SHORT HE CANNOT KEEP PACE WITH THE OTHERS.

I SHALL GOAD HIM ON.

*SARPA! SARPA!

WHEN NAHUSHA KICKED HIM, AGASTYA BECAME ANGRY.

HOW DARE YOU! SARPO BHAVA** MY CURSE WILL TURN YOU INTO A SNAKE.

* MOVE ON. ALSO SNAKE.   30   ** MAY YOU BECOME A SNAKE.

SUBSCRIBE NOW!

Pay only ₹~~360~~ 290!

19% OFF

A twelve month subscription to
TINKLE MAGAZINE

YOUR DETAILS*

Student's Name _____

Parent's Name _____

Date of Birth: _____ (DD MM YYYY)

Address: _____

_____

_____

City: _____ PIN: _____

State: _____

School: _____

Class: _____

Email (Student): _____

Email (Parent): _____

Tel of Parent: (R): _____

Mobile: _____

_____
Parent's Signature:
*All the above fields are mandatory for the subscription to get activated.

PAYMENT OPTIONS

☐ **Credit Card**
Card Type: Visa ☐ MasterCard ☐
Please charge ₹290 to my Credit Card Number
below: ☐☐☐☐ ☐☐☐☐ ☐☐☐☐ ☐☐☐☐
Expiry Date: ☐☐ ☐☐

_____
Cardmember's Signature:

☐ **CHEQUE / DD**
Enclosed please find cheque / DD no. ☐☐☐☐☐☐ drawn in
favour of "ACK Media Direct Pvt. Ltd."
on (bank)_____,
for the amount _____, dated ☐☐/☐☐/☐☐☐☐ and
send it to: **IBH magazine Service, Arch no.30, Below
Mahalaxmi Bridge, Near Racecourse, Mahalaxmi,
Mumbai 400034**

☐ **Pay by VPP**
Please pay the ₹290 to the postman on the delivery
of 1st issue. (Additional charges ₹30 apply)

☐ **Online subscription**
Visit www.amarchitrakatha.com

For any queries or further information please
write to us ACK Media Direct Pvt. Ltd.,
Krishna House, 3rd Floor, Raghuvanshi Mills Compund,
Senapati Bapat Marg, Lower Parel, Mumbai 400 013.
Tel: 022-40 49 74 36
or send us an Email at customercare@ack-media.com

SAVITRI

THE PERFECT WIFE

www.amarchitrakatha.com

The route to your roots

SAVITRI

Even the merciless Lord Yama is charmed by Savitri. This gentle, beautiful princess is admired by gods and kings, the rich and the poor, the young and the old. But when the shadow of death hangs over her husband she is filled with courage spurred by her selfless love for him. She strives for a miracle – with amazing success!

<table>
<tr><td align="center">**Script**
Anant Pai</td><td align="center">**Illustrations**
Ram Waeerkar</td><td align="center">**Editor**
Anant Pai</td></tr>
</table>

Cover illustration by: Pratap Mulick

SAVITRI

LONG AGO, IN THE KINGDOM OF MADRA RULED A KING CALLED ASVAPATI. HE WAS A RIGHTEOUS KING.

HE HAD MANY WIVES – AS WAS THE CUSTOM IN THOSE DAYS. THE PALACE ECHOED WITH THEIR HAPPY VOICES.

BUT ASVAPATI WAS UNHAPPY. HE HAD NO CHILDREN.

WHY ARE YOU SAD, YOUR MAJESTY?

I HAVE WORSHIPPED THE GODS BUT STILL HAVE NO CHILD.

YOUR MAJESTY! I HAVE HEARD GOD SAVITR FULFILS MANY WISHES!

SAVITR? THEN I SHALL GO TO HIS TEMPLE.

ANY NEWS?

DO YOU THINK IT WILL BE A BOY?

IN THE PALACE, LATER —

GO, TELL THE KING! IT'S A GIRL.

YOUR MAJESTY! A PRINCESS HAS BEEN BORN!

AT LAST!

THE WHOLE KINGDOM REJOICED. THE KING GAVE AWAY CLOTHES AND JEWELS.

LONG LIVE OUR PRINCESS!

I SHALL CALL HER SAVITRI AFTER THE GOD SAVITR.

THE PALACE WAS FILLED WITH THE CHILD'S LAUGHTER.

YOU BRING UP A DAUGHTER AND ONE DAY SHE LEAVES FOR ANOTHER HOME!

GIRLS ARE LIKE FLOWERS! WHEREVER THEY GO, THEY MAKE THE WORLD BEAUTIFUL!

AS SHE GREW UP, SAVITRI LEARNT MUSIC, PHILOSOPHY...

...AND ASTRONOMY...

DO STARS RULE OUR FATE?

...THEN TO THE GROWING GIRL CAME THE KNOWLEDGE OF PAIN... OF SEPARATION.

FATHER! MY FRIENDS SAY A GIRL MUST MARRY AND GO AWAY! I WILL NOT GO ANYWHERE!

HA! HA! IT'S NOT TIME YET FOR THAT, MY DEAR!

BUT TIME PASSED... SAVITRI HAD GROWN TO BE A BEAUTIFUL WOMAN. ONE DAY SHE CAME TO HER FATHER.

FATHER! MAY I GO TO THE TEMPLE?

ALL ALONE? WELL, YES! YOU ARE OLD ENOUGH!

IN THE QUIET STILLNESS OF THE TEMPLE SITUATED ON A HILL TOP, SAVITRI'S HEART WAS FILLED WITH HAPPINESS.

WHY DIDN'T I COME HERE BEFORE?

ON HER WAY BACK SAVITRI SAW A GROUP OF YOUNG OFFICERS RIDING NEAR THE PALACE GATE.

GOOD DAY, PRINCESS!

WHY DID YOU BOW YOUR HEAD TO ME?

BECAUSE YOU ARE OUR PRINCESS!

WERE SHE NOT A PRINCESS, I'D STILL BOW BEFORE ONE SO BEAUTIFUL!

SAVITRI OVERHEARD THE REMARK OF THE YOUNG OFFICER AND BLUSHED RED IN THE FACE.

SUCH BEAUTIFUL HORSES!

COME, SAVITRI, WE'RE GETTING LATE!

THE KING HAD WATCHED THE INCIDENT FROM THE PALACE WINDOW.

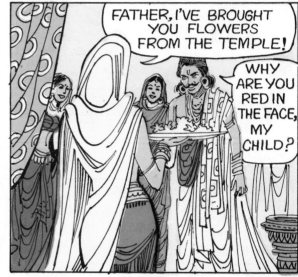

FATHER, I'VE BROUGHT YOU FLOWERS FROM THE TEMPLE!

WHY ARE YOU RED IN THE FACE, MY CHILD?

LOOKING AT THE RECEDING FIGURE OF HIS DAUGHTER, THE KING REALISED HOW BEAUTIFUL SHE HAD BECOME.

OH! IT'S THE SUN OUTSIDE!

I MUST FIND A HUSBAND FOR HER.

NEWS OF SAVITRI'S BEAUTY AND LEARNING HAD REACHED OTHER ROYAL COURTS.

THE MADRA KING'S DAUGHTER IS ELIGIBLE FOR MARRIAGE!

LOOK AT MY SONS! HOW CAN YOU THINK OF SUCH A MATCH?

ANOTHER KING'S COURT—

NO, NOT MY SON! A LEARNED WOMAN LIKE HER DESERVES SOMEONE BETTER!

IT WAS THE SAME STORY EVERYWHERE...

THE PRINCE HAS GROWN UP. SHALL WE APPROACH THE KING OF MADRA?

YOU MEAN SAVITRI? NO, I DON'T THINK WE CAN DO HER HONOUR!

...NO ONE DARED ASK FOR SAVITRI'S HAND.

HAVE WE RECEIVED ANY PROPOSALS FOR SAVITRI?

NO, YOUR MAJESTY!

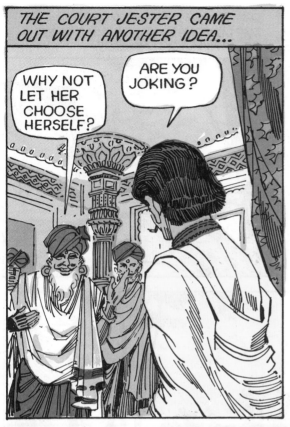

THE COURT JESTER CAME OUT WITH ANOTHER IDEA...

WHY NOT LET HER CHOOSE HERSELF?

ARE YOU JOKING?

THE KING LIKED THE IDEA. HE CALLED SAVITRI TO HIS ROOM. SAVITRI WAS RELUCTANT.

I DON'T WISH TO MARRY! WHY DO YOU WANT TO SEND ME AWAY?

IT IS SAID, A FATHER, WHO DOES NOT GIVE HIS DAUGHTER IN MARRIAGE, IS A SINNER.

ALL RIGHT, FATHER! I SHALL DO WHAT YOU SAY.

IT WAS ARRANGED THAT SAVITRI WOULD GO ON A TRIP THROUGH MANY KINGDOMS, THE MINISTER WOULD ACCOMPANY HER.

LOOK FOR A HUSBAND WHO WILL BE YOUR EQUAL.

SAVITRI WAS THRILLED WITH THE JOURNEY— SHE WOULD VISIT SO MANY HOLY PLACES.

WHILE PASSING THROUGH A FOREST, THEY SAW A YOUNG HERMIT WALKING BY THE SIDE OF THE ROAD.

SAVITRI'S EYES FELL ON THE YOUNG MAN'S FACE AND SHE FELT A STRANGE EMOTION.

SO YOUNG, AND YET A HERMIT?

THE FACE WAS IMPRINTED ON HER MEMORY.

TOMORROW WE SHALL BE THE GUESTS OF THE KING OF VARANASI!

AT VARANASI—

MY SONS ARE BRAVE AND STRONG! YOU MAY MAKE YOUR CHOICE, MY CHILD.

FOR SAVITRI, A CHANCE MEETING HAD DIMMED THE REST OF THE WORLD.

HAVE YOU MADE YOUR CHOICE?

NO! LET'S GO BACK HOME!

WHAT KIND OF A MAN DO YOU WANT FOR A HUSBAND?

HOW CAN I TELL HIM? I DON'T EVEN KNOW HIS NAME!

THE CHARIOT PASSED THROUGH THE FOREST AGAIN. SAVITRI SENSED THAT SHE WOULD MEET HIM AGAIN.

I AM THIRSTY! CAN WE STOP FOR SOME WATER?

I SEE A COTTAGE THERE! I'LL GO AND SEE!

SOON SHE WAS STARTLED BY A WARM YOUTHFUL VOICE...

MAY I GIVE SOME WATER TO THE PRINCESS?

YES, IT'S HE! BUT HE IS A HERMIT! HOW CAN I...?

SAVITRI KNEW SHE HAD TO KNOW THE TRUTH! SHE COULD NOT GO AWAY.

PLEASE STOP! FIND OUT WHO HE IS! EVERYTHING!

ALL RIGHT! I'LL GO!

SOON THE MINISTER RETURNED.

HE IS NO HERMIT! HIS NAME IS SATYAVAN, SON OF AN EXILED KING. BUT, IS HE YOUR CHOICE?

YES!

AT LAST SAVITRI RETURNED TO HER FATHER'S PALACE. THE KING CAME OUT TO GREET HER...

COME HOME MY DAUGHTER! HAVE YOU MADE YOUR CHOICE?

YES, FATHER!

BUT SAVITRI WAS SOON OVERCOME WITH EMBARRASSMENT...SHE COULD NOT SPEAK...

WHY DO YOU BLUSH, MY DEAR?

SHE HAS CHOSEN SATYAVAN! HE LIVES IN THE FOREST.

IN THE FOREST?

...BUT THE CONVERSATION WAS SOON INTERRUPTED.

YOUR MAJESTY! SAGE NARADA SEEKS YOUR AUDIENCE!

OH! I MUST GO AND WELCOME HIM!

WHAT IS THIS LITTLE CONFERENCE ABOUT?

MY DAUGHTER HAS CHOSEN A POOR MAN FOR HER HUSBAND! HIS NAME IS SATYAVAN!

SATYAVAN?

WHY DID SHE HAVE TO CHOOSE HIM?

THE KING HAD SEEN THE LOOK OF SADNESS IN NARADA'S EYES.

DO YOU KNOW HIM?

YES! HIS FATHER DYUMATSENA WAS KING OF SALVA! AFTER HE BECAME BLIND, HE LOST HIS KINGDOM!

THEN WHY ARE YOU SILENT? IS IT BECAUSE THEY LIVE IN THE FOREST NOW?

NO, NOT THAT!

HOW CAN I TELL HIM THE REAL REASON!

ASVAPATI KEPT ON ASKING THE SAGE.

IS HE NOT NOBLE? IS HE NOT BRAVE?

HE IS THE NOBLEST AND BRAVEST OF ALL!

FINALLY NARADA HAD TO COME OUT WITH THE TRUTH.

HE IS DESTINED TO DIE EXACTLY ONE YEAR FROM TODAY.

THAT MEANS MY CHILD WILL BE A WIDOW IN A YEAR?

YES! IF SHE MARRIES HIM!

ASVAPATI WAS VERY UPSET. HE CALLED SAVITRI.

MY CHILD! YOU CANNOT MARRY SATYAVAN! HE IS GOING TO DIE SOON!

BUT FATHER! I'VE ALREADY CHOSEN HIM WITH MY HEART! HOW COULD I MARRY ANYONE ELSE?

AT LAST, ASVAPATI HAD TO GIVE IN.

YOUR DAUGHTER HAS MADE A BRAVE CHOICE! PLEASE ACCEPT IT!

YES! I'LL ACCEPT IT!

ONE DAY SOON AFTER, A BRIDAL PROCESSION REACHED THE FOREST...
THE HERMITS CAME FORWARD TO RECEIVE AND WELCOME THEM.

AT FIRST, DYUMATSENA WAS HESITANT.

YOUR CHILD HAS LIVED IN WEALTH! HOW CAN SHE BE HAPPY HERE?

PLEASE DO NOT WORRY! SHE HAS CHOSEN SOMETHING GREATER THAN WEALTH!

HER FRIENDS DRESSED SAVITRI BEAUTIFULLY.

HAVE YOU SEEN THE GROOM? HE IS SO HANDSOME!

ONLY FOR ONE YEAR!

YES!

CHANTING THE SACRED MANTRA OF MARRIAGE, ASVAPATI GAVE AWAY HIS DAUGHTER TO SATYAVAN.

THE BRIDE AND GROOM WALKED AROUND THE SACRED FIRE SEVEN TIMES. THEY WERE MARRIED NOW.

THEN IT WAS TIME FOR FAREWELL.

BE PROUD OF YOUR CHOICE AND BE HAPPY!

AS SOON AS HER PARENTS LEFT, SAVITRI TOOK OFF ALL HER JEWELS AND CLOTHED HERSELF IN CLOTHES OF BARK.

WHY ARE YOU DRESSED LIKE THIS?

YOU ARE A HERMIT! I AM YOUR WIFE! HOW ELSE SHOULD I BE DRESSED?

SATYAVAN TOOK OUT A BEAUTIFUL RING HE HAD KEPT FOR HER.

YOU MUST WEAR THIS! SEE THE STONE! IT IS POLISHED AND YOU CAN SEE YOUR FACE IN IT!

LIKE A MIRROR? BUT WHY SHOULD I NEED A MIRROR?

YOU HAVE A BEAUTIFUL FACE. LOOK AT IT!

SAVITRI WAS EXTREMELY DEVOTED TO HER PARENTS-IN-LAW! SHE LOOKED AFTER THEM LIKE A DUTIFUL DAUGHTER.

IT'S LATE, MY CHILD! YOU MUST GO TO BED!

IS THERE ANYTHING ELSE I CAN DO?

AS THE DAYS PASSED, A SECRET AGONY GREW WITHIN HER HEART.

WHAT DAY IS IT TODAY, MOTHER?

THE EIGHTH DAY AFTER THE NEW MOON!

ONLY SIXTY DAYS MORE!

AT LAST, THE YEAR WENT BY. THREE DAYS BEFORE THE FATE-FUL DAY, SAVITRI BEGAN FASTING.

BUT, MY CHILD! THIS IS TOO HARD A PENANCE!

PLEASE DO NOT WORRY, FATHER! I CAN DO IT!

ON THE LAST NIGHT SHE COULD NOT SLEEP. ONLY ONE THOUGHT KEPT ON HAUNTING HER.

TOMORROW MY HUSBAND IS FATED TO DIE! WHAT SHALL I DO?

IN THE MORNING—

PLEASE LET ME GO WITH YOU TODAY.

WHY SAVITRI?

I JUST WANT TO GO!

ALL RIGHT, COME WITH ME!

HER SMILING FACE HID THE AGONY IN HER HEART. SATYAVAN WAS HAPPY...

BUT YOU MUST WEAR YOUR ANKLETS! I WANT TO HEAR YOUR FOOTSTEPS!

IN THE FOREST, SAVITRI'S HEART WAS FULL OF ANGUISH.

THE WORLD IS BEAUTIFUL! BUT·LIFE IS TOO SHORT TO APPRECIATE EVERYTHING!

SAVITRI! WHY DO YOU HAVE SUCH SAD THOUGHTS?

SAVITRI RAN TOWARDS HER HUSBAND...

SAVITRI, MY LIMBS ARE LOSING ALL SENSATION! LET ME SLEEP FOR A WHILE!

SOON, SATYAVAN'S BODY BECAME STILL.

SO THIS IS THE END?

THE FOREST AROUND HER HAD DARKENED... A HEAVY STILLNESS FILLED THE AIR... SAVITRI LIFTED HER HEAD AND SAW A DARK FIGURE CLAD IN RED, A CROWN SHINING ON HIS HEAD.

SAVITRI WAS TROUBLED, BUT SHE FELT NO FEAR. SHE WANTED TO SPEAK TO HIM...

WHO ARE YOU?

HAVEN'T YOU GUESSED? I AM YAMA, GOD OF DEATH. I'VE COME FOR SATYAVAN'S SOUL!

MY LORD! I'VE HEARD, YOUR ASSISTANTS DO THIS JOB. WHY HAVE YOU COME YOURSELF?

SATYAVAN WAS NO ORDINARY PERSON. HE WAS PURE. THAT'S WHY I HAVE COME!

YAMA TOOK OUT A SMALL NOOSE. HE SLIPPED IT AROUND SATYAVAN'S BODY AND STARTED BACK.

SAVITRI SAW THAT SATYAVAN'S FACE HAD ASSUMED THE STILLNESS OF A CORPSE.

MY BELOVED HUSBAND IS DEAD! I HAVE NOTHING LEFT NOW IN LIFE! LET ME FOLLOW LORD YAMA!

SAVITRI FOLLOWED YAMA FROM A DISTANCE! THE TALL SOFT GRASS OF THE FOREST MUFFLED THE SOUND OF HER ANKLETS.

SOON THEY CAME UPON A STREAM. HERE TOO THE WATER SOFTENED THE SOUND OF HER FOOTSTEPS.

ON THE HARD GROUND, HER ANKLETS FILLED THE AIR WITH A MOURNFUL SOUND...

...WHICH SOON REACHED YAMA'S EARS! THE GOD OF DEATH PAUSED TO LISTEN TO THE STRANGE SOUND.

SOMEONE SEEMS TO BE FOLLOWING ME!

YAMA WAS ASTONISHED THAT SAVITRI DID NOT ASK ANYTHING FOR HERSELF.

YOU MUST GO BACK NOW! YOU CAN'T COME ANY FARTHER.

IN LIFE AND DEATH I AM WEDDED TO HIM! I HAVE TO FOLLOW HIM!

BUT HE IS LYING THERE IN THE FOREST. YOU SHOULD ARRANGE FOR HIS FUNERAL!

WHY DO YOU TEST ME? WHAT GOOD IS THE BODY WHEN THE SOUL LEAVES IT?

SAVITRI'S WORDS FILLED THE AIR LIKE SOLEMN MUSIC. EVEN YAMA'S STEPS HAD SLOWED DOWN.

YOUR HUSBAND'S LIFE IS ALREADY TAKEN! I AM PLEASED WITH YOUR DEVOTION! ASK FOR TWO MORE BOONS!

SAVITRI KNEW SHE COULD NOT ASK FOR SATYAVAN'S LIFE DIRECTLY! BUT SHE FOUND A WAY!

MY FATHER HAS NO SONS TO CARRY ON HIS LINE! WILL YOU GRANT HIM SONS?

IT WILL BE DONE! WHAT ELSE DO YOU ASK?

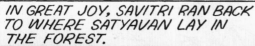 IN GREAT JOY, SAVITRI RAN BACK TO WHERE SATYAVAN LAY IN THE FOREST.

HE WAS LYING THERE AS SHE HAD LEFT HIM, STILL, MOTIONLESS. SAVITRI HAD A DOUBT.

IS HE REALLY ALIVE? WHY CAN'T I SEE HIM BREATHE?

SAVITRI KNEW THAT A POLISHED STONE BECOMES MISTY WITH A MAN'S BREATH. SHE TOOK OFF HER RING AND HELD IT NEAR HIS NOSE.

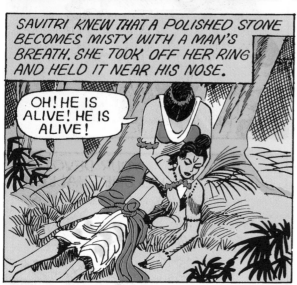

OH! HE IS ALIVE! HE IS ALIVE!

SATYAVAN SOON OPENED HIS EYES.

HOW LONG HAVE I BEEN SLEEPING?

THE HAPPY COUPLE STARTED FOR THEIR HOME! SAVITRI'S HEART WAS FILLED WITH HAPPINESS.

A HUNDRED SONS, HE SAID!

MEANWHILE... DYUMATSENA HAD GOT BACK HIS SIGHT.

WHY ARE YOU LOOKING AT ME LIKE THAT?

BECAUSE I CAN SEE YOU! IT'S A MIRACLE! MY WIFE!

BUT WHERE IS MY SON, SATYAVAN? WHERE IS SAVITRI? THEY SHOULD HAVE COME BACK BY NOW.

AS THE WORRIED DYUMATSENA STEPPED OUTSIDE, HE SAW A STORM CLOUD AT THE EDGE OF THE FOREST.

IS THAT A STORM APPROACHING?

NO, IT LOOKS LIKE HORSE-MEN TO ME!

THE HORSEMEN SOON ARRIVED! DYUMATSENA RECOGNISED THEM. THEY CAME FROM HIS LOST KINGDOM.

YOUR MAJESTY! THE ENEMIES HAVE BEEN DEFEATED! WE HAVE COME TO TAKE YOU BACK.

ANOTHER MIRACLE!

THE EXILES STARTED FOR THEIR KINGDOM.
IT WAS A JOYOUS JOURNEY FOR ALL.

THE EXILES STARTED FOR THEIR KINGDOM.
IT WAS A JOYOUS JOURNEY FOR ALL.

SUBSCRIBE NOW!

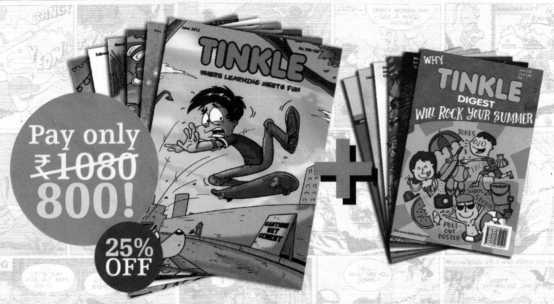

Pay only ₹~~1080~~ 800!

25% OFF

A twelve month subscription to
TINKLE and TINKLE DIGEST

YOUR DETAILS*

Student's Name _____

Parent's Name _____

Date of Birth: _____ (DD MM YYYY)

Address: _____

_____

_____

City: _____ PIN: _____

State: _____

School: _____

Class: _____

Email (Student): _____

Email (Parent): _____

Tel of Parent: (R): _____

Mobile: _____

_____
Parent's Signature:

*All the above fields are mandatory for the subscription to get activated.

PAYMENT OPTIONS

☐ **Credit Card**
Card Type: Visa ☐ MasterCard ☐
Please charge ₹800 to my Credit Card Number
below: ☐☐☐☐ ☐☐☐☐ ☐☐☐☐ ☐☐☐☐
Expiry Date: ☐☐ ☐☐

_____
Cardmember's Signature:

☐ **CHEQUE / DD**
Enclosed please find cheque / DD no. ☐☐☐☐☐ drawn in favour of "ACK Media Direct Pvt. Ltd."
on (bank)_____
for the amount _____, dated ☐☐/☐☐/☐☐☐☐ and
send it to: **IBH magazine Service, Arch no.30, Below Mahalaxmi Bridge, Near Racecourse, Mahalaxmi, Mumbai 400034**

☐ **Pay by VPP**
Please pay the ₹800 to the postman on the delivery
of 1st issue. (Additional charges ₹30 apply)

☐ **Online subscription**
Visit www.amarchitrakatha.com

For any queries or further information please
write to us ACK Media Direct Pvt. Ltd.,
Krishna House, 3rd Floor, Raghuvanshi Mills Compund,
Senapati Bapat Marg, Lower Parel, Mumbai 400 013.
Tel: 022-40 49 74 36
or send us an Email at customercare@ack-media.com